Quiet Profits in Briar Hollow

The Quiet Discretion Mysteries - Book Two

Petra Shaw

CSD Digital Enterprises, LLC

A Note to the Reader

Welcome to **Briar Hollow**.

This is a **cozy mystery series** set in a small town where secrets tend to linger—and sometimes, objects remember what people try to forget.

Each book in this series features:

A **complete mystery solved by the end of the story**

A **quiet paranormal element** rooted in intuition and emotional echoes—not visions, prophecies, or dark magic

A curious amateur sleuth, a watchful talking cat, and a town that prefers its truths kept tidy

No graphic violence, no explicit content, and no gore

While there is an ongoing thread connecting the series, **every book stands on its own** and can be enjoyed independently.

These stories are written for readers who enjoy:

Atmospheric, character-driven mysteries

Small towns with complicated histories

Gentle suspense rather than shock

Cozy pacing with thoughtful reveals

If you enjoy mysteries that unfold quietly, reward attention, and leave room for reflection after the final page, you're in the right place.

Now, step inside.

Series Introduction

A Note on These Stories

The Quiet Discretion Mysteries are set in small towns where nothing is quite as simple as it looks.

These are not stories about villains hiding in the dark or secrets uncovered through force. They are about what happens when people mean well, systems move carefully, and silence starts being treated as agreement.

Clara Whitlock does not investigate crimes in the usual way. She listens. She waits. She notices what others overlook—not because they are hiding, but because no one has asked the right question yet.

Each book in this series stands on its own, but together they follow a larger pattern: how authority forms, how harm is disguised as care, and what it costs to refuse escalation when escalation would be easier.

If you're looking for loud twists or fast judgments, these stories may feel different.

If you're interested in quiet tension, moral pressure, and the consequences of choosing restraint, you're in the right place.

Series Introduction

A Note on These Stories

[illegible]

[illegible]

[illegible]

[illegible]

[illegible]

[illegible]

Contents

Chapter One

Hush Money in Briar Hollow

The ledger smelled like old leather and dust.

Clara Whitlock noticed that before she noticed the woman holding it.

The bell over the door chimed just after lunch, a careful, apologetic sound that matched the posture of the woman stepping into *Second Chances Antiques*. She hesitated on the threshold as if the shop itself might object to her presence, then crossed the floor with slow, deliberate steps, a canvas tote clutched tightly to her chest.

Nimbus lifted his head from his post in the front window. His yellow eyes narrowed to sharp slits.

"Oh," he said quietly. "That's not a cookbook."

Clara didn't reach for the tote. She didn't even smile yet. Experience had taught her that certain objects—and the people who carried them—needed acknowledgment before contact. Rushing either usually ended poorly.

"Hi," the woman said. Her voice carried the faint strain of someone who'd rehearsed the moment and still hadn't settled on the right tone. "I was told you might be able to tell me if this is... anything."

Clara nodded and gestured to the counter. "Why don't you start by telling me where it came from."

The woman hesitated, then set the tote down as if it were heavier than it looked. "My uncle's house. He passed last week. Heart, they said." She made a vague motion with her hand, as if hearts were faulty appliances rather than organs. "I'm clearing things out. There's... a lot."

"I'm sorry," Clara said, and meant it.

The woman shrugged, but the motion didn't reach her eyes. "He was complicated."

Nimbus snorted. "They always are."

Clara shot him a warning look and reached for her gloves—thin cotton, folded neatly beneath the counter. Habit now. Professionalism. Or fear that had learned to behave itself.

When she opened the tote, the ledger sat right on top.

No attempt to hide it. No careful wrapping. Just a battered leather book with a cracked spine and softened corners, the kind of thing that had been handled often and intentionally. A bent clasp hung loose at the side, its hinge worn thin, as if someone had worried it open and shut more times than they cared to admit.

Clara didn't touch it yet.

The feeling pressed in anyway.

Not panic. Not grief. Just tightness.

Counting.

A controlled, persistent tally, like fingers tapping against a tabletop while someone waited for a confirmation that never quite arrived.

Clara kept her breathing slow and even. "Did you ever see him use this?"

The woman shook her head. "No. He kept it in a drawer. Locked." Her brow furrowed. "Which is strange. He didn't lock anything else."

Nimbus hopped onto the counter and leaned closer, nose twitching. "Locked drawers are where people keep the parts of themselves they don't want audited."

Clara slipped on her gloves and lifted the ledger.

The echo sharpened immediately.

Anxiety—controlled, practiced. Numbers lining up with mechanical precision. Relief, brief and almost pleasant. Then something threaded through it all, thin but unmistakable.

Fear.

Clara's jaw tightened.

She opened the ledger.

The pages were yellowed but meticulously neat, the handwriting precise to the point of obsession. Dates marched down the left margin. Amounts stood to attention on the right. Short notes filled the narrow space between them.

Consulting.

Permit assistance.

Fee.

Nothing illegal at first glance. Nothing dramatic. Language designed to survive scrutiny.

But the rhythm was wrong.

Too regular. Too careful. Too consistent to be casual.

Nimbus leaned in. "That's not spending."

Clara turned a page. Then another. "It's maintenance."

Initials repeated across the paper. Sometimes three letters. Sometimes two. Occasionally just one. Familiar shapes without names attached.

"Do these mean anything to you?" Clara asked, keeping her tone neutral.

The woman leaned forward, squinting. "No. I never saw this before."

Clara closed the book gently. "I'll need some time to research it."

The woman exhaled with visible relief. "That's fine. If it's nothing, you can toss it."

Nimbus's gaze snapped up. "People never say that unless they're hoping you won't."

Clara met the woman's eyes steadily. "I won't toss it."

The woman swallowed, nodded once, and left quickly—too quickly—like someone relieved to be done with the asking.

When the door closed, the shop felt quieter than before.

Nimbus stretched. "So. Who's been paying whom to sleep at night?"

Clara traced one gloved finger along the ledger's edge. "Someone who thought this solved a problem."

Nimbus's tail flicked. "And then stopped."

Clara's phone buzzed on the counter.

The display said: **June (Diner):** You hear about Carl Benton?

Clara's stomach dipped.

Carl Benton owned half the commercial properties on the south end of town. He sponsored parades, cut ribbons, and smiled like nothing ever cost him anything.

She typed back.

Clara: No. What happened?

The dots appeared. Disappeared. Appeared again.

June: Found him this morning. In his recliner. Looked peaceful.

Clara closed her eyes.

Nimbus didn't speak.

Clara set the ledger down, the neat rows of numbers suddenly heavier than paper had any right to be.

Peaceful deaths didn't usually arrive with ledgers full of quiet payments.

She locked the book in the cabinet beneath the counter and slid the key into her pocket, the familiar weight grounding her.

Nimbus watched her carefully. "Tell me you're not thinking what I think you're thinking."

Clara met his gaze. "Someone just lost their income."

Nimbus sighed. "And now they're motivated."

Outside, Briar Hollow carried on with its afternoon errands, already practicing the word *natural* in lowered voices.

Inside, Clara stood very still, listening to the silence the ledger left behind.

It wasn't empty.

It was keeping count.

Chapter Two

Amounts Owed

Briar Hollow had a way of turning death into punctuation.

A pause.

A lowered voice.

A casserole wrapped in foil and expectation.

Carl Benton's death earned all three before sunset.

By the time Clara unlocked *Second Chances Antiques* the next morning, the town had already decided what kind of story it wanted.

Peaceful. Natural. Sad, but not disruptive.

Those words floated through the square like fallen leaves—light enough to drift anywhere, heavy enough to cover what people didn't want to see underneath.

Clara heard Carl's name twice before she even turned the sign to *Open*. Once from a woman walking a golden retriever who slowed as she passed the shop window. Once from an older man buying picture frames who said it in the careful, even tone reserved for weather updates.

"Peaceful, they say," the man added, as if peace were a favor Carl Benton had finally done the town.

Clara nodded, rang him up, and locked the door behind him with a little more force than necessary.

Nimbus hopped onto the counter and flicked his tail like a metronome keeping time with Clara's irritation. "I hate that word."

"Which one?" Clara asked, even though she knew.

"Peaceful," Nimbus said. "It's what people say when they don't want to ask follow-up questions."

Clara pressed her palms flat on the counter and breathed in slowly—wood polish, old paper, lemon oil. Familiar scents. Safe scents. Her shop did not usually smell like rumors. This week, it did.

"That's how Briar Hollow survives," Clara said.

Nimbus blinked, unimpressed. "That's how Briar Hollow avoids accountability."

Clara didn't argue, because Nimbus was irritatingly correct more often than was healthy.

Her phone rang.

She didn't need to look at the screen to guess. Halden never called to chat, and no one else had the sense to call before nine.

"Clara Whitlock," she answered.

"Clara." Sheriff Halden's voice was level, familiar, and faintly tired. "You hear about Benton?"

"Yes."

"Good. Saves me some explaining." Paper rustled on his end, like he was already building the official version in a file folder. "Natural causes, most likely. He had a known heart condition."

Clara leaned her hip against the counter, gaze drifting—without meaning to—to the cabinet beneath it. "Most likely."

There was a small pause. Not a reaction. Just the quiet recognition of a hesitation he chose not to name.

Halden didn't push. "You told me you'd flag anything odd."

"I did," Clara said carefully. "And I will."

Another pause. Longer this time.

"You sound tired," Halden said.

"I am."

"So am I," he replied, and the admission landed with more weight than the words themselves. "If you notice anything relevant—anything at all—you call me."

"I will," Clara said again.

They hung up without ceremony. No comfort. No warning. Just a line drawn between what could be said out loud and what couldn't.

Nimbus watched her set the phone down. "He's waiting."

"He's listening," Clara corrected.

Nimbus's ears twitched. "That's worse."

Clara turned the sign to *Open* out of habit. She lasted twelve minutes. One customer came in, browsed the glass case without seeing anything, and left without buying so much as a postcard. The town wasn't shopping today. It was processing. And processing in Briar Hollow meant talking in low voices, not spending money.

Clara flipped the sign to *Closed* again.

"Ah," Nimbus said. "The economy of grief."

Clara ignored him, knelt, and unlocked the cabinet.

The ledger waited exactly where she'd left it—silent, patient, smug in its neatness.

She set it on the counter and took a breath before opening it. The echo returned immediately. Less sharp than yesterday, but persistent: anxiety humming beneath the surface, numbers lining up, a relief that never lasted long enough to feel safe.

Clara flipped to the last page.

One entry stood alone.

C.B. — 3,000 — final

Her pulse ticked up.

Nimbus leaned forward. "Final," he read. "That's not a delay. That's a door slamming."

Clara traced the date with her gloved fingertip. Two weeks ago.

She flipped back a few pages.

The same initials.

The same amount.

Month after month, like clockwork.

"Three thousand dollars," Clara murmured. "Enough to matter. Not enough to draw attention."

Nimbus's tail flicked. "Comfort money."

"Silence money," Clara said.

She leaned closer, scanning the margins. Faint notes sat beside several entries—words written small enough to pretend they were nothing.

Delay.

Handled.

Hold.

Clara felt a chill settle between her shoulders.

"This wasn't bribery," she said slowly. "Not the loud kind. This was... maintenance."

Nimbus nodded. "Payments made to keep problems from becoming conversations."

Clara turned pages, careful and steady. The handwriting never changed. The rhythm never broke. Whoever kept this ledger had been consistent in the way only anxious people could be.

She flipped to the front.

There it was.

Not initials. Not coded.

Carl Benton — Primary

Her breath caught.

Nimbus stared at the page. "Primary payer."

"Yes," Clara said quietly. "Which means Carl wasn't being paid."

"He was paying," Nimbus finished. "And now he's dead."

Clara closed the ledger, the sound soft but final.

Outside, a car rolled past, its tires whispering on cold pavement. A dog barked once and fell silent. Life continued with its usual disinterest in human secrets.

Clara stared at the ledger as if it might explain itself.

"If someone killed Carl to keep this quiet," she said, "it wasn't because he was talking."

Nimbus hopped down from the counter and began pacing the length of the glass case, nails clicking softly like a countdown. "It's because he stopped."

Clara nodded, the conclusion settling like a stone.

She locked the ledger back in the cabinet and slid the key deeper into her pocket, as if distance could stop the implications from spreading.

She didn't go for her coat. She didn't turn the sign back to *Open*.

Instead, she stood behind the counter, listening to her shop and the town beyond it.

"Tomorrow," Nimbus said, voice dry, "you'll go ask questions."

Clara's mouth tightened. "Tomorrow I confirm what I already suspect."

Nimbus paused and looked at her. "And today?"

"Today," Clara said, "I stop pretending this is just bookkeeping."

Nimbus blinked slowly. "That's the spirit."

Clara turned off the lights she didn't need and looked once more at the cabinet under the counter.

The ledger didn't feel like a relic anymore.

It felt like a trigger.

Behind her, the shop settled into silence.

But the numbers in the ledger didn't rest.

They waited.

Chapter Three

What the Town Calls Peace

The pressure didn't arrive all at once.

It came in polite pieces.

Clara noticed it first at the post office.

She'd stopped in midmorning, more out of habit than necessity, and was standing in line behind Mrs. Calder when the woman turned, smiled too brightly, and said, "Such a shame about Carl."

Clara nodded. "It is."

Mrs. Calder leaned closer, lowering her voice as if grief itself were confidential. "But at least it was peaceful."

There it was again.

Peaceful.

Clara felt Nimbus's presence at her ankle, solid and warm.

"That word is working overtime," he murmured.

Mrs. Calder continued, clearly relieved to have found a listener. "Carl did so much for this town. Jobs. Sponsorships. Donations. It would be awful if people started... questioning things."

Clara kept her expression neutral. "Questioning what?"

Mrs. Calder blinked, surprised. "Oh. You know. *Things.*" She laughed lightly, the sound brittle. "No sense dragging it out. That doesn't help anyone."

The clerk called Mrs. Calder forward, and the conversation dissolved as neatly as it had formed.

Nimbus looked up at Clara. "That wasn't concern."

"No," Clara said quietly. "That was instruction."

The second push came at the diner.

June slid Clara her usual mug—hot water, cinnamon stick—then hesitated instead of moving away.

"You stirring something up?" June asked, not unkindly.

Clara looked up. "Why would you ask that?"

June wiped the counter, already clean. "People are talking. Not loudly. But they're talking." She paused. "They don't like surprises."

Nimbus snorted. "They love secrets, though."

June glanced at the empty stool beside Clara and shivered. "Tell me you're being careful."

"I am," Clara said.

June nodded, not reassured. "Good. Because the word going around is *closure.*"

Clara frowned. "That's not a bad word."

"It is when it's being used as a lid," June said. "People want this done. Tidy. No loose ends."

Clara watched a man at the counter laugh a little too hard at nothing. "Loose ends make people nervous."

"They make people angry," June corrected.

Nimbus leaned closer to Clara's ear. "Anger wrapped in politeness is still anger."

By noon, the pressure had sharpened.

A woman browsing teacups asked, "You're not getting involved in all that unpleasantness, are you?"

A man buying a lamp said, "Best thing for Briar Hollow is to let things settle."

A delivery driver joked, "You've always had a knack for finding old junk. Just don't go digging up anything that should stay buried."

Each comment came with a smile.

Each smile carried the same message.

Stop.

Clara locked the shop early.

She stood behind the counter, hands braced against the wood, breathing through the weight of it. The town wasn't threatening her. It didn't need to.

It was reminding her where she lived.

Nimbus jumped onto the counter and paced. "They're afraid."

"Of what?" Clara asked.

"Of mirrors," Nimbus said. "Of losing the version of themselves where nothing ugly ever happened unless it was an accident."

Clara stared at the door. "They think I'm making it worse."

Nimbus stopped pacing. "They think you're making it visible."

That landed harder.

Clara exhaled slowly. "I didn't ask for this."

Nimbus flicked his tail. "Neither did Carl. But he's still dead."

A knock came at the door.

Not the bell.

A knock.

Clara froze.

Nimbus went utterly still.

"Clara?" called a familiar voice. "It's just me."

She recognized it—Tom Willis, head of the Chamber of Commerce. He stood outside smiling through the glass like a man practicing reassurance.

Clara unlocked the door but didn't invite him in.

Tom stepped just inside, hands raised slightly as if he were calming a skittish animal. "I won't take much of your time."

Nimbus muttered, "They never do."

Tom glanced around the shop. "You know, this place is such an asset to Briar Hollow. Quirky. Charming. People come here to feel comfortable."

Clara didn't respond.

Tom cleared his throat. "We've all had a rough couple of days. Emotions are high. Folks are just hoping things can return to normal."

"What's normal?" Clara asked.

Tom smiled wider. "Quiet."

There it was—said outright at last.

Clara met his gaze. "Quiet isn't the same as right."

Tom's smile tightened. "No one's asking you to do anything improper."

"Then what are you asking?" Clara said.

Tom hesitated, recalibrating. "Discretion."

Nimbus bared his teeth. "Ah. The polite word for silence."

Clara shook her head. "I don't sell discretion."

Tom's smile faltered. "Clara—"

"I sell objects," she said. "And sometimes the truth that clings to them."

A long beat passed.

Tom exhaled. "Just... be careful. Briar Hollow takes care of its own."

Clara watched him leave without replying.

When the door shut, the shop felt heavier than before.

Nimbus looked up at her. "That was the town asking nicely."

Clara nodded. "And if I say no?"

Nimbus's eyes gleamed. "Then they'll stop being nice."

Clara squared her shoulders.

"Then I won't be quiet," she said.

Nimbus smiled, sharp and proud. "Good. Neither will the ledger."

Chapter Four

Who Stops Getting Paid

Morning came sharp and bright, the kind of cold that made Briar Hollow look clean even when it was slightly untidy.

Frost webbed the edges of the shop windows, turning the glass into something between lace and warning. Clara unlocked the front door just after eight, and the bell chimed with its usual politeness—too cheerful for a town that had spent the last twenty-four hours practicing *natural causes* like it was a prayer.

She stepped inside and let the familiar smells wrap around her: cedar, lemon oil, old paper, faint dust warmed by yesterday's sun. The shop was quiet in the way it always was before customers arrived, but today that quiet felt tense—like the room was waiting for her to make a mistake.

Nimbus paused on the threshold with one paw lifted, head tilted, as if he could read the mood in the air.

"It still smells like money," he said. "And not the good kind."

Clara hung her coat on the hook. "There is no good kind."

Nimbus blinked slowly. "You say that, and yet you keep accepting it from strangers."

Clara ignored him and went straight to the cabinet under the counter. She didn't let herself hesitate this time. Hesitation was how panic snuck in.

She unlocked the cabinet, pulled out the ledger, and set it on the counter where the morning light could hit it full-on. The cracked leather looked drier today. Less menacing. More like an exhausted animal that had carried too much weight for too long.

She opened to the front.

Carl Benton — Primary

The words sat there with infuriating calm.

Clara stared for three seconds—just long enough for the reality of it to settle again. Carl Benton, town benefactor and commercial landlord, had been paying someone. Regularly. Quietly. For years, if the thickness of the ledger meant what she thought it meant.

Nimbus hopped onto the counter and leaned over the page, whiskers twitching. "Let's be methodical," he said. "Who needed Carl alive?"

Clara flipped to the most recent pages. "People he paid."

"And who needed him quiet?" Nimbus asked, tone dry.

Clara didn't look up. "Probably the same people."

Nimbus's tail flicked once. "Which means the secret isn't the problem."

"The money is," Clara finished.

She pulled a notepad from under the counter and began copying initials. Four sets that repeated most often. She didn't try to decode them yet; she didn't have to. The pattern mattered more than the names at this stage.

She circled the last two weeks with a heavy pen stroke.

"Two weeks ago," she murmured, "everything changes."

Nimbus leaned closer. "That's when someone stopped getting paid."

"And panicked," Clara said.

She forced herself to slow down. Not because she wasn't sure, but because rushing made her sloppy—and sloppy was how people got hurt in small towns. She flipped back three months and checked again.

Same rhythm. Same amounts. Same careful language in the notes.

Then the sudden word: **final**.

Not delayed. Not reduced. Not renegotiated.

Stopped.

Clara tore the page from the notepad and folded it into quarters, tucking it into her coat pocket like a secret she could carry without letting it leak. She didn't trust leaving it on the counter, not with the shop's front door and its too-friendly bell between her and the world.

Nimbus tracked her movement. "Where are we going?"

"The diner," Clara said.

Nimbus's ears perked. "Ah. Bacon truths."

Clara rolled her eyes. "People talk around food."

"They talk around coffee too," Nimbus said. "But you don't drink it, so we do bacon."

Clara grabbed her coat and locked the shop behind them.

The Briar Hollow Diner was already half-full. The air inside was warm and greasy in the comforting way only diners managed—fried potatoes, butter, sugar, and the steady drip of conversation that never truly stopped.

The bell on the diner door chimed as Clara stepped in, and she felt the tiniest shift in attention. Not a full turn of heads, but a slight quieting of voices. Carl Benton's name had turned the town into an animal listening for predators.

June spotted her immediately and poured a mug without asking. Clara didn't drink coffee, and June knew it, so she filled it with hot water and slid a small tin of cinnamon sticks along with it.

Clara's gratitude tightened her throat. "Thanks."

June leaned in, voice low. "You look like you're hunting."

Clara wrapped her hands around the warmth. "I have questions."

June snorted softly. "So does everyone. They just pretend they don't."

Clara kept her gaze on the counter, not on the customers. People didn't like being watched while they talked. "Did Carl change his routine lately?"

June's expression shifted—subtle, but real. "He stopped paying his tab."

Clara blinked. "Stopped?"

"Two weeks ago," June said. "Not like he couldn't afford it. Like he suddenly decided he didn't want to."

Nimbus, perched invisibly on the stool beside Clara, murmured, "That's your cut-off."

June continued, lowering her voice. "He paid cash that day—clean, exact amount, no tip—then said he was 'tightening things up.' After that, he didn't come in. Not once."

Clara's stomach tightened. "Carl Benton didn't miss breakfast."

June shook her head. "He missed nothing. He was a habit in a jacket. That's why it felt... wrong."

Clara nodded slowly. "Did he meet anyone here recently?"

June hesitated, then glanced toward the kitchen. When she looked back, her eyes were sharper. "Last Friday. Booth by the window."

"Who?" Clara asked.

June exhaled. "You didn't hear it from me."

Clara didn't rush her. She let the silence do its job.

Finally, June said, "Lydia Marsh. County permits. She comes in sometimes, always with a folder, always counting her cash twice before she pays. Nervous energy."

Nimbus went still. "That tracks."

Clara's pulse picked up. "What were they talking about?"

June leaned closer. "I only caught pieces. Carl said something like, 'I'm done paying for peace.' Lydia said, 'You can't just stop.'"

The words slid into place so neatly Clara almost hated them.

"Did Carl get angry?" Clara asked.

June shook her head. "No. He smiled. That's what bothered me. He had this... satisfied look. Like he'd finally decided something, and nobody could talk him out of it."

Clara's mind flashed to the word **final** in the ledger.

June watched her. "Clara... what are you doing?"

Clara didn't lie. She just didn't answer fully. "Making sure 'peaceful' means what they want it to mean."

June's face softened. "Be careful."

Clara left a few bills on the counter—more than the water was worth—and June pretended not to notice while still sliding them neatly into the tip jar like she didn't want the gesture to become a conversation.

Outside, the cold slapped Clara's cheeks awake again.

Nimbus padded beside her, tail low but purposeful. "Permit office," he said.

Clara nodded. "Permit office."

The County Permit Office was a squat brick building designed to discourage lingering. The lobby smelled like toner and old carpet, and the fluorescent lights were unforgiving in the way government buildings always were—bright enough to expose everything, warm enough to comfort nothing.

Clara signed in, waited, and listened to the bored rhythm of a wall clock that sounded too much like counting.

Lydia Marsh sat behind a desk stacked with folders. Her posture was rigid, her hair pulled back tight, glasses perched low on her nose. She looked up when Clara approached, surprise flickering across her face before it snapped into polite professionalism.

"Can I help you?" Lydia asked.

Clara smiled pleasantly, the way she did with difficult customers. "I hope so. I'm researching some old permits tied to Carl Benton."

Lydia's fingers paused over the keyboard.

"I'm not sure why that would concern—" she began.

"He died yesterday," Clara said gently.

The air changed.

Lydia swallowed. "Yes. I heard."

Clara's gaze drifted—not to Lydia's face, but to the objects on her desk. A pen worn thin from use. A stapler with a dented corner. A clean rectangle of space where something ledger-sized had obviously been moved recently.

Nimbus's voice dropped. "She's already afraid."

Clara pulled out her gloves. Lydia noticed immediately.

"What are you doing?" Lydia asked, a little too quickly.

"Being careful," Clara said. "I handle old items. It's habit."

Lydia's gaze tracked the gloves like they were suspicious in their own right. Clara didn't explain further. Explanation invited questions, and questions invited attention she didn't want.

Clara reached for the pen.

The echo hit her with clean precision.

Relief—short-lived.

Calculation—steady, practiced.

Fear—sharp and immediate.

And beneath it, the thought that pressed forward with startling clarity:

I needed that money.

Clara kept her face calm. She met Lydia's eyes.

"You were being paid to smooth things over," Clara said quietly. "Permits. Delays. Quiet approvals."

Lydia shook her head too fast. "That's not—"

"Carl stopped," Clara continued. "Two weeks ago."

Something in Lydia's face broke—just a hairline fracture at first, then a widening crack. "He said it wasn't personal," she whispered. "He said the development was done. He said there was no reason to keep—"

"To keep paying," Clara finished softly.

Lydia's shoulders slumped. "I didn't hurt him," she said, voice shaking. "I just went to talk."

Nimbus's tail lashed. "And?"

Clara didn't push harshly. She didn't need to. The truth was already trying to escape.

"What happened next?" Clara asked.

Lydia swallowed hard. "We argued. Not loud. Just... tense. He stood up like he was done with me. He grabbed his chest." Tears spilled before Lydia seemed to realize they were coming. "I thought it was the heart thing. I thought he'd sit back down. I thought he'd—"

Clara's throat tightened. "And you didn't call for help."

Lydia's breath hitched. "I froze."

"Because you were scared," Clara said.

"Yes," Lydia sobbed. "I thought it would come back to me. The payments. The ledger. Everything. I didn't—" She pressed a hand to her mouth. "I didn't want to be the reason everyone looked at me."

Nimbus's voice was quiet now. "And so, you became the reason anyway."

Clara exhaled slowly. "Sheriff Halden will need to hear this."

Lydia nodded, defeated, like she'd been holding the truth under water and finally couldn't anymore.

"I know," she whispered. "I know."

Clara stepped back from the desk, the pen still in her gloved hand like a small, ordinary witness.

Outside the permit office, the cold air felt cleaner. Not kinder—just clearer.

Nimbus looked up at Clara. "Money stopped. Silence didn't."

Clara tucked her hands into her coat pockets, gloves and all. "It never does."

Behind them, the county building hummed with its fluorescent indifference, papers stacked and stamped and filed like they were the only things that mattered.

In Briar Hollow, someone had decided numbers were safer than truth.

Clara had just proven they weren't.

Chapter Five

What Counts as Quiet

Sheriff Halden didn't look surprised.

That was the first thing Clara noticed when Lydia Marsh finally stopped talking long enough to breathe.

He sat behind his desk with his sleeves rolled up, pen resting loosely between his fingers, posture calm in a way that said he'd heard every version of fear people could offer and still expected the truth to fit inside it. His office smelled faintly of paper and winter air—someone had opened a window earlier, as if fresh cold could rinse the room clean.

Lydia sat across from him, shoulders hunched, eyes swollen and red. Her hands twisted together in her lap like they were trying to wring out what she'd done.

Clara stood off to the side—close enough to be part of it, far enough to be sure she wasn't steering it. She kept her face neutral and her hands still. This wasn't her role now. This was the part where the town's quiet habits met something official and unforgiving.

Nimbus sat on the narrow credenza beneath the window, tail wrapped tight around his paws, watching Halden with interest.

"That's a man who hates paperwork but loves clarity," he murmured.

Halden closed his notebook with a soft, final sound.

"You didn't intend to kill him," Halden said evenly, voice low but firm. "But you created the conditions that led to his death. And you chose not to call for help."

Lydia's lips trembled. "I was afraid."

Halden didn't raise his voice. He didn't have to. "Fear explains things. It doesn't excuse them."

He stood and gestured toward the door. "We'll continue this downtown."

Lydia rose slowly, like her legs didn't trust the floor. She didn't resist. Resistance would've required believing there was still a version of this where she didn't end up in trouble.

She glanced once at Clara. Not anger. Not accusation. Just that bleak, sick realization that a private decision had become a public consequence.

Then she walked out with Halden.

When the door shut, Clara felt the office exhale. The silence afterward was different—cleaner. Not peaceful, but not vibrating anymore.

Halden returned a moment later, alone. He set the folder on his desk and looked at Clara with a kind of exhausted professionalism.

"You brought me something solid," he said.

Clara kept her voice careful. "I brought you a pattern."

Halden's mouth tightened like he didn't like the word *pattern* because it implied this wasn't the first, and wouldn't be the last. "That too."

He studied her for a beat. "You didn't bring the ledger in, did you?"

"No," Clara said. "It's locked up."

Halden nodded once. "Good. I'll need it logged." He paused, then added, "And Clara—don't tell me how you found your pattern. I'm not asking. That's on purpose."

Clara's throat tightened. "Understood."

Nimbus's tail flicked. "He's building a little shelf in his brain labeled *Don't Ask Whitlock.*"

Halden reached for another paper in his folder. "Carl Benton's autopsy confirmed stress-induced cardiac failure. Triggered by confrontation."

Clara let out a slow breath she hadn't realized she'd been holding. "So, it wasn't staged."

"No," Halden said. "Just pressured." His eyes held hers. "That doesn't make it harmless."

Nimbus murmured, "Pressure kills more cleanly than knives."

Halden didn't react to the cat's voice, but his gaze sharpened as if he felt the same truth without needing words. "This town has a habit of smoothing things over," he said. "Today, it doesn't get to."

Clara nodded. "Thank you."

Halden gave a rough little laugh. "Don't thank me yet. People don't like losing their shortcuts."

He walked her to the door, then stopped with his hand on the knob. "If anyone comes sniffing around your shop—anyone you don't recognize—call me."

Clara's pulse ticked up. "You mean besides the usual sniffers."

Halden's expression didn't shift much, but there was a grim humor in his eyes. "Besides them."

By the time Clara returned to *Second Chances Antiques*, the afternoon light had shifted. Sun angled through the front window, turning dust motes into floating sparks. The shop looked harmless from the outside—just a cozy little place full of forgotten things. But Clara had learned that forgotten didn't mean safe.

She unlocked the door and stepped in.

Nimbus jumped onto the counter and immediately took his position facing the street, like a sentry. "If we're being watched," he said, "I'd like them to feel judged."

Clara set her keys down. "You do that naturally."

Nimbus's ears twitched. "Thank you."

Clara went to the cabinet and retrieved the ledger. She didn't open it. Not now. She didn't need its echo to confirm what she already knew: money had been flowing, then stopped, and someone had panicked hard enough to let a man die.

She wrapped the ledger in brown paper again, tied it with twine, and set it under the counter for Halden to collect.

Nimbus watched her hands. "You see the pattern yet?"

Clara paused. "Silence costs something."

Nimbus nodded once. "And eventually, someone can't afford it."

The bell over the door chimed.

Clara's head snapped up.

A man stood just inside the entrance—mid-thirties, neat jacket, shoes too clean for the icy slush outside. His smile was polite and practiced, the kind that didn't waste energy. His eyes moved across the shelves without truly seeing the objects, like he was evaluating the room rather than shopping in it.

"Afternoon," he said. "I'm looking for something specific."

Clara returned the smile, every instinct tightening. "What's that?"

"Things that tell stories people don't want told."

Nimbus's fur lifted along his spine. "That's not a customer."

Clara stayed behind the counter. No stepping forward. No inviting tone. “You’re looking for a different kind of shop.”

The man’s smile widened just a fraction. “So, it seems.”

He didn’t argue. He didn’t ask for her name. He didn’t pretend to browse. He simply held her gaze for a long beat—measuring, curious—then nodded like he’d confirmed what he came to confirm.

He turned and left.

The bell chimed again, cheerful and wrong.

Clara stood very still.

Nimbus stared at the door. “That,” he said, “is going to be a problem later.”

Clara swallowed. “He wasn’t from town.”

Nimbus’s tail flicked. “No. And he wasn’t surprised either.”

Clara looked down at the wrapped ledger under the counter.

The money trail was done.

The confession was recorded.

But someone had noticed the way it ended.

And that kind of attention never came quietly.

Chapter Six

What Doesn't Stay Buried

The man didn't come back.

Clara told herself that should have been a relief.

It wasn't.

Briar Hollow had patterns. Predictable ones. People circled the same questions, the same rumors, the same grudges, until everything either dissolved into boredom or hardened into certainty. Strangers, especially, rarely did anything once. They checked a place. They checked a person. Then they checked again.

This man had walked in, said the kind of sentence that didn't belong in a normal antique shop, and left like he'd only needed to confirm she existed.

Then he vanished.

Nimbus spent most of the afternoon posted in the front window, body still, eyes active, tail occasionally ticking with displeasure. He watched every person who passed like he was evaluating whether they had a motive, an alibi, or a conscience.

"That one's lying to someone," he said as an older woman hurried across the street with a leather bag.

Clara, rearranging a display of china cups that had already been arranged twice, didn't look up. "How can you tell?"

Nimbus's ears twitched. "She's walking like she's late to a conversation."

A teenager cut across the square, hood up, hands jammed deep into pockets.

Nimbus's tail flicked once. "That one's stealing something. Probably not from you, but still."

Clara sighed. "You're exhausting."

Nimbus didn't blink. "I'm accurate."

Clara tried to keep the shop open as normal. She really did. She flipped the sign to *Open*, straightened the brass lamps, polished the glass case, and pretended she was just a woman with a quirky shop and a moody cat.

But the day refused to behave.

Customers came in, browsed without seeing, and left empty-handed. When they spoke, they spoke in that careful, coded way small towns used when tragedy sat too close.

"Such a shame," one woman murmured, lifting a porcelain bird only to set it back down as if it were suddenly fragile.

"Yes," Clara said, because that was the only safe response.

"Oh, and—did you hear?" the woman added, eyes flicking toward the door like gossip could be arrested.

Clara did not ask what she'd heard. She didn't need to.

By early afternoon, the diner down the street sent the smell of fried potatoes drifting through the square. The town's metabolism shifted—lunch, chatter, an attempt to keep going.

Clara watched it all through her front window and felt the strange disconnect of being both inside and outside at once.

Nimbus jumped down from the window and padded behind the counter, brushing against her ankle with the casual possessiveness of a creature who did not ask permission to belong.

"You're spiraling," he said.

"I'm working," Clara replied.

Nimbus's eyes narrowed. "You're pretending that if you keep your hands busy, your head will stop counting."

Clara froze, cloth in hand. "I don't—"

Nimbus hopped onto the counter. "You do. You count risks. You count exits. You count how long it's been since the bell rang. You're practically a ledger yourself."

Clara's throat tightened. She set the cloth down slowly. "I don't like being watched."

Nimbus's ears angled forward. "Then stop acting like you're alone."

The bell over the door chimed.

Clara's entire body tightened before she could stop it.

But it wasn't the stranger. It was Sheriff Halden.

He stepped inside without ceremony, coat collar turned up against the cold, face drawn in the way it got when he'd spent the day cutting through people's excuses.

Nimbus's tail flicked. "Ah. The human with the badge."

Halden didn't glance at Nimbus, but his eyes landed on Clara and held. "You all right?"

Clara forced herself to breathe. "I'm aware."

Halden gave a faint, humorless smile. "That's usually how it starts."

He moved to the counter. "I'm here for the ledger."

Clara nodded and reached under the counter to retrieve the wrapped bundle. Brown paper, twine. Evidence disguised as something ordinary.

Halden took it carefully, and Clara watched his hands—gloved, steady. He was the type of man who respected objects the way he respected guns: not because they were sacred, but because they were dangerous when misunderstood.

"Lydia Marsh is being booked," Halden said. "Voluntary manslaughter. Failure to render aid."

Clara's stomach dipped anyway. The charge wasn't a shock, but the finality of it was.

"And Carl?" she asked.

Halden exhaled through his nose. "Official cause stands. Stress-induced cardiac failure. Triggered by confrontation." He paused. "It doesn't look clean on paper. But it's the truth."

Nimbus's voice was low. "Truth rarely flatters anyone."

Halden glanced toward the window, toward the street. "Town's already trying to decide what this means."

Clara's mouth tightened. "What do they want it to mean?"

Halden's eyes narrowed slightly. "They want it to mean it's over."

Clara didn't respond. She didn't trust herself to say what she was thinking—that in Briar Hollow, *over* was just the word people used when they were tired.

Halden shifted the ledger under one arm. "You hear from anyone... unusual... you call me."

Clara's pulse ticked up. "I had a man come in earlier."

Halden's posture sharpened. "Describe him."

Clara did—clean jacket, too-alert eyes, wrong kind of smile, wrong kind of question.

Halden's jaw tightened. "You didn't get a name."

"No."

"License plate?"

"No."

Nimbus sighed. "We're bad at surveillance."

Halden held her gaze. "If he comes back, you call immediately. You don't engage."

Clara nodded. "Understood."

Halden paused at the door, hand on the knob. He didn't soften his voice, but it lowered slightly. "Clara."

She looked up.

"Briar Hollow doesn't like mirrors," he said. "You're holding one up. That makes people... unpredictable. They don't like seeing themselves as they really are."

Clara swallowed. "I'm not trying to—"

"I know," Halden said, and there was something almost kind in the way he said it. "Still. Be careful."

Then he left.

The bell chimed cheerfully behind him, as if the shop hadn't just absorbed another warning.

Clara locked the door immediately after he was gone, even though it wasn't closing time yet.

Nimbus watched her. "You're closing early."

"I'm thinking," Clara said.

Nimbus hopped down to the floor and sat, looking up at her. "And what do you think?"

Clara stared at the street through the glass. People passed. Cars rolled by. Life continued with its practiced indifference.

"I think," she said slowly, "that the ledger wasn't the only thing someone was keeping track of."

Nimbus's eyes gleamed. "There it is."

Clara turned the sign to *CLOSED* and killed the overhead lights, leaving only the softer lamps glowing around the shop. Shadows gathered in the corners, making the antiques look like they were listening.

She breathed once, twice, trying to convince her body it was safe.

The bell chimed.

Both of them froze.

The door did not open.

Something slid across the threshold and stopped at Clara's feet with a soft scrape.

A small parcel.

No knock.

No voice.

No footsteps retreating.

Just the package, placed like a message.

Nimbus's fur rose along his spine. "No."

Clara didn't touch it right away. She crouched slowly, studying it where it lay, as if it might suddenly move on its own.

Brown paper, neatly wrapped. Twine tied tight. No return address. One word written in careful ink, all caps like a label.

FOR WHITLOCK

Her throat tightened.

Nimbus's voice dropped to a whisper. "That's not coincidence."

Clara slipped on her gloves with shaking hands—not dramatic shaking, but controlled. The kind of shaking that came from adrenaline being told it had to behave.

She lifted the parcel.

It wasn't heavy, but it had weight—the kind that came from intent.

She carried it to the counter and set it down gently, like something sleeping.

She didn't open it.

Not yet.

Nimbus stared at it like it had personally offended him. "Whatever that is," he said, "it's not from town."

Clara swallowed. "No."

Outside, Briar Hollow hummed with evening sounds—cars, laughter from the diner, a radio playing too loud somewhere it shouldn't. The town was already trying to normalize what had happened, smoothing the edges, rewriting the discomfort into something easier to swallow.

Inside, Clara stood very still behind her counter.

Because silence had a cost.

And someone—somewhere—had decided she was worth paying attention to.

She turned the sign to **CLOSED** (again, as if it could seal the door against intention), reached for the light switch, and let the shop fall into deeper shadow.

Tomorrow, she'd open the package.

Tonight, she let it wait.

Chapter Seven

What the Quiet Leaves Behind

The town didn't say thank you.

Clara hadn't expected it to.

Two days after Lydia Marsh was taken into custody, Briar Hollow adjusted its posture the way it always did—shoulders back, chin up, eyes forward. The story settled into place with a new vocabulary: *unfortunate*, *misunderstanding*, *stress*. The sharper words were quietly retired.

Clara watched it happen from behind the counter at *Second Chances Antiques*.

Customers returned slowly, cautiously, like animals testing whether a storm had truly passed. They browsed. They chatted. They avoided looking directly at her for too long.

Nimbus lay stretched across the front window, tail flicking occasionally. "They've decided you're safe again," he said.

"For how long?" Clara asked.

Nimbus cracked one eye open. "Depends on whether you keep reminding them."

Clara adjusted a display of old postcards—scenes of Briar Hollow from decades past. Smiling people. Empty streets. A version of the town that had never existed as neatly as the photographs suggested.

The bell chimed.

Vesta Rowe stepped inside.

She looked smaller than the last time Clara had seen her, grief pressing her inward like weather. She hesitated near the door, hands clenched around her purse strap.

Clara came out from behind the counter. "You don't have to—"

"I wanted to," Vesta said quickly. "Before I talked myself out of it."

They stood there for a moment, surrounded by objects that had survived longer than most regrets.

"I know people are saying things," Vesta said. "About Carl. About what he did. About what Lydia did." Her jaw tightened. "I don't care."

Clara waited.

Vesta met her eyes. "He wasn't perfect. He was... controlling. Careful. Always trying to make problems go away with money." She swallowed. "But he didn't deserve to die like that."

"No," Clara said softly. "He didn't."

Vesta exhaled shakily. "Thank you for not letting them pretend it was nothing."

Clara felt the weight of that land. "It wasn't nothing."

Vesta nodded once, satisfied, and left without another word.

Nimbus watched the door close. "That one mattered."

Clara leaned against the counter, suddenly tired in a way sleep didn't fix.

That afternoon, Sheriff Halden stopped by without warning.

He didn't stay long.

"Paperwork's done," he said. "Charges are official."

Clara nodded. "And the town?"

Halden's mouth twitched. "Already rewriting itself."

Nimbus snorted. "Talented like that."

Halden hesitated. "I wanted you to know... some people are unhappy."

Clara met his gaze. "I assumed."

"But," Halden continued, "some people are relieved." He paused. "They just won't say it out loud."

Clara absorbed that quietly.

Halden moved toward the door, then stopped. "About the man you mentioned."

Clara's pulse ticked up. "Yes?"

"I asked around," Halden said. "No one recognizes him. No plates caught. No record of him in town that day."

Nimbus's fur bristled. "Of course not."

Halden looked at Clara seriously. "That doesn't sit right with me."

"It doesn't sit right with me either," Clara said.

Halden nodded once. "Just... don't go looking for trouble."

Clara didn't promise.

That evening, after the shop was closed and the town lights softened into their nighttime glow, Clara stood alone behind the counter.

The parcel sat where she'd left it.

Unopened.

Nimbus watched her from the stool. "You're still not going to open it, are you?"

"Not tonight," Clara said.

"Good," Nimbus replied. "Anticipation is educational."

Clara smiled faintly. "You're enjoying this."

Nimbus's eyes gleamed. "I enjoy preparedness."

Clara reached out and rested her hand—not on the parcel, but on the counter beside it. She didn't need to touch it to feel its presence. Pride. Intention. Expectation.

Someone had seen what she did.

Not the town.

Not the sheriff.

Someone else.

Clara squared her shoulders.

She hadn't asked to become a mirror.

But she wouldn't look away now that she was one.

Nimbus hopped down and brushed against her leg. "You're going to keep doing this."

Clara nodded. "Yes."

Nimbus's tail flicked. "Good. Because quiet never stays quiet forever."

Clara turned off the last light, leaving the parcel in shadow.

Tomorrow would come with questions.

Tonight, she let the truth sit where it belonged—acknowledged, uncomfortable, and impossible to ignore.

Continue the Quiet Discretion Mysteries

Briar Hollow doesn't stay quiet for long.

If you enjoyed *Quiet Profits in Briar Hollow*, the story continues immediately in the next installment of **The Quiet Discretion Mysteries**, where a new object, a new secret, and a new silence demand attention.

Each book in the series features a complete mystery, while Clara Whitlock's story unfolds quietly in the background.

Continue with **Book Three:** ***Bloodline Blush in Briar Hollow***

Reading Order

Book One: Dead Quiet in Briar Hollow

Book Two: Quiet Profits in Briar Hollow

Book Three: Bloodline Blush in Briar Hollow

Book Four: Quiet Inheritance in Briar Hollow

Book Five: Quiet Custodian in Briar Hollow

Book Six: Quiet Fractures Beyond Briar Hollow

Book Seven: Quiet Consent Beyond Briar Hollow

Book Eight: Quiet Clippings in Briar Hollow

Book Nine: Quiet Verdict in Briar Hollow

Book Ten: The Cost of Quiet in Briar Hollow

Book Eleven: No Neutral Ground in Briar Hollow

Book Twelve: No More Quiet in Briar Hollow

The next chapter of the Quiet Discretion Mysteries is already unfolding.

A Small Favor

If you enjoyed this story, a brief review makes a real difference.

Reviews help other readers find cozy mysteries they'll enjoy—and they help authors continue writing them. Even a sentence or two is appreciated.

Thank you for reading.

https://www.amazon.com/review/create-review/?ie=UTF8&channel=glance-detail&asin=B0GC4NC3H1

About the author

Petra Shaw writes quiet, character-driven cozy mysteries with a gentle paranormal edge.

Her stories are set in small towns where secrets linger, objects hold memories, and truth often waits for someone willing to notice what others overlook. With a focus on atmosphere, intuition, and understated suspense, Petra's books favor thoughtful mysteries over shock—and resolution over chaos.

When she isn't writing, Petra can usually be found imagining new towns, new silences, and the next mystery waiting just beneath the surface.

Petra Shaw

www.ingramcontent.com/pod-product-compliance
Lightning Source LLC
La Vergne TN
LVHW040221110826
845146LV00005B/1373

* 9 7 9 8 9 9 4 4 2 7 8 1 1 *